GRANDPA'S GARDEN

In memory of my Grandpa, William Hubert Woodyard,
and to Kathryn and J. P. Montgomery,
for taking up where he left off. — *Shea Darian*

To three generations of very special women in my life,
my mother Lucille, my daughter Renee,
and my granddaughter Brianna. — *Karlyn Holman*

Published by DAWN Publications
14618 Tyler Foote Road
Nevada City, CA 95959
916 292-3482

Library of Congress Cataloging-in-Publication
(Prepared by Quality Books, Inc.)

Darian, Shea, 1959-
Grandpa's garden / Shea Darian ; illustrated by Karlyn Holman/
p. cm.
ISBN: 1-883220-42-4 (hardback)
ISBN: 1-883220-41-6 (paperback)

I. Holman, Karlyn, ill. II. Title.

PZ7.D375Gran 1996   [E]
QBI95-20655

Printed on recycled paper using soy based ink

Printed in Hong Kong

10 9 8 7 6 5 4 3 2 1
First Edition

Designed by LeeAnn Brook Design
Type style is Caslon 540

A Note from the Author

Gardens have been places of wonder to me for as long as I can remember. It all started with my grandfather, who welcomed me to such a patch of land—a garden which, for me, held as much wisdom and beauty as any place on earth. For in my Grandpa's garden I learned first-hand of the life and death, the growth and change of which a garden speaks.

For Grandpa and me, his garden was a place we shared our deepest feelings, thoughts, and wishes. It was a place I harvested the goodness of Grandpa's humor and wisdom about life, which has proven its usefulness over many years. I hope Grandpa's Garden and the gardening celebrations that follow will inspire you and those you care for to see gardens as places where love and wisdom can grow alongside the vegetables, fruits, and flowers.

On Saturdays I work in Grandpa's garden.

Here with the peas and turnips,

we talk about the mysteries of life:

why Ms. Fowler (who lives around the corner) always wears her sunbonnet off kilter,

how a pole bean finds its climbing pole,

and why my older brother never seems to see me anymore,

now that Alice Maken smiles at him when he says hello.

On Saturdays I work in Grandpa's garden.
Here with the strawberries and tomatoes,
I tell him things that no one knows but him and me:
that one day I want to be a great actor, or the world's fastest runner,
and that one day I want to make friends with the deaf girl down the street.

On Saturdays I work in Grandpa's garden.

Here with the radishes and lettuce,

and the garden fairy who's lived here since I can remember.

We pretend the fairy grants us each three wishes.

I wish to find a four-leaf clover, to learn to skate backwards,

and to have three more wishes.

He wishes for a jar of homemade preserves,
that his corn will grow healthy and tall,
and that when he gets to heaven, just once,
he can get a glimpse of
"our Maker's face,
full of love and shinin'
like the sun."

On Saturdays I work in Grandpa's garden.

The heat of the sun makes sweat beads under our straw hats.

I watch Grandpa's face, fix in my mind the color of his eyes,

the wrinkles that come when he laughs,

and the way he folds his bandanna after he wipes the sweat away.

Some days we do not speak.

Grandpa says words are like shiny new dimes—

you should ask yourself if they're better off spent or sittin' in your pocket.

So we dig and plant, hum and sway,

and keep our words for another day.

Grandpa is like an old work horse.

Grandma says he never knows when to stop.

But one day he stops before the sun is high in the sky.

He stops long before I am tired or sweaty.

Grandpa sits down hard on an old sawed-off tree stump.

He grabs his arm and scrunches his face.

I run down the gravel drive like the wind,
yellin' for Grandma to come quick.
Everything happens so fast, the ambulance comes,
and Grandpa goes off to the hospital.
Grandma says his heart isn't working right,
that he needs to rest for a time until his heart is strong again.

On Saturdays I work in Grandpa's garden,
here without the soft hum of Grandpa's voice,
the voice that feeds the plants as much as the earth and sun and rain.
There is much to do, and Grandma says while Grandpa has his rest
she is looking to me to keep the weeds from taking over,
and to harvest the food when it is ready.
Sometimes I cry when I think of how much I miss Grandpa,
but Grandma says that is just fine
because my tears will feed the garden too.

The weather has been hot and dry,

so I take some compost from the pile Grandpa calls the "earthworm's delight."

I spread it around each plant the way Grandpa taught me,

and water the plants with the garden hose.

As I spray the garden, it glistens and drinks down the water.

In the misty spray, I can almost see Grandpa here with me.
He moves about the garden with his bushel basket,
gathering radishes and peas, spinach and turnips.
In my mind, he pulls up a radish, shakes it a bit, and sets it in my open hand.
He winks and tells me, "A little dirt never hurt anybody."
I smile, and pop the radish in my mouth, like an adventure.

On Saturdays, I work in Grandpa's garden.
Turning compost with a shovel,
I remember Grandpa saying troubles are like garbage in the
compost heap—scraps of food, dead leaves, dry grass.
Mix it all up and after a time that old smelly stuff
turns into good, rich food for the plants.
"Troubles are the compost of life," Grandpa would say,
"if you have patience to see what they turn into,
you see what first appears to be a trouble
can also be a gift.
Over time, troubles have a way
of makin' us healthy and strong."

Grandma tells me Grandpa is getting stronger,
and that tomorrow we'll go to the hospital for a visit.
I smile as I pick the first ripe tomatoes of the summer
and in my mind I hear Grandpa say, "Looks like a mighty fine year for tomatoes."
"Yes, Grandpa," I tell him, "And look at your corn, silky tops showin' already."

The next day I do some weeding in the garden.
Then I wash up "in a snap," as Grandpa would say,
and drive to the hospital with Grandma.

In Grandpa's room, he takes my hand and kisses it.
"Well, I almost got my wish this time," he says, "to see that face in heaven. . .
but no sight is more welcome to these old eyes than this little face."
Grandpa's eyes are shining as I hand him flowers from the garden.
I tell him how straight and tall his corn has grown.
He smiles, and says in a few days he'll see it for himself.

On Saturdays I work in Grandpa's garden,

here with Grandpa standing beside me again, healthy and tall like the corn.

We sing as we harvest the first ears of the season.

We pick cucumbers and gather beans.

Then we sit to rest, and I tell him how scared I was that he might not come back.

Grandpa says every day is a gift, and that I don't need to worry about him dying.

He says he is certain he will die one day, and then his wish will come true—

to get a glimpse of our Maker's face, full of love and shinin' like the sun.

On Saturdays I work in Grandpa's garden.

Here with the spiders and worms, we work long into the afternoon.

A pesky bee stings my ankle,

and I hop up and down, yelping like a puppy.

Grandpa picks some mint leaves from the patch by the house.

He chews up a few and lays them on my ankle,

tending to me carefully with his strong, wrinkled old hands.

On Saturdays I work on Grandpa's Garden.
The weeks pass by, and we harvest the plenty.
The smell of autumn is in the air,
and Grandpa is an old workhorse again.
We'll pull carrots and dig up rutabagas.

As we work, Grandpa tells me that life is like a garden,
sown with tiny seeds.
He says there is a season for growing, a season for harvesting,
and a season for letting the soil rest.
And I know it's true—for every autumn
Grandpa and I put the garden to sleep for the winter.
But it is not time for that yet.

Then after dinner, as we often do,
Grandpa and I sit by the garden to welcome the evening.
We listen to the crickets, and watch the sun spread out with its blanket of colors.
In the quiet, I figure Grandpa's wish has already come true.
For when I look into Grandpa's eyes, I see
a glimpse of that face already glowing there—
the one so full of love and shinin' like the sun.

Listening in the Garden

Mother Earth is our teacher, sharing with us important lessons about life.
To understand her, we learn to listen not only with our ears, but also with our eyes, hands and
hearts. There is no better place to hear these lessons than in the garden, which overflows with the
wonder and wisdom of our Mother, the Earth.

Listen to Mother Earth, here in the garden. Come quietly from time to time.

Through the quiet perhaps Mother Earth will speak of the soil as her skin—

in some places worn thin, in others, many inches deep.

Soil—made of tiny pieces of broken rock, dead plants and creatures

changed into earth by the powers of the wind, rain, ice and air.

Soil—which sometimes takes hundreds of years to become even

one inch of the covering for Mother Earth.

Soil—out of which grows the food for all the creatures of the world.

Mother Earth asks us to walk gently upon the soil, to remember always to

care for it as if our lives depend upon it—because all life does.

Listen to Mother Earth, here in the garden. Come quietly from time to time.

Through the quiet, perhaps Mother Earth will speak of the wonder of

seeds, such tiny flakes, little balls and oblong shapes no bigger than the tip of a finger.

Seeds—called the "keepers of secrets" for keeping their secrets all winter long.

Seeds—that seem dead as we hold them in our hands, yet they are

the tiny, humble homes of a bounteous harvest.

Seeds—which when planted will be coaxed by earth, rain, and sun

to grow into plants hundreds, thousands, even millions of times larger.

Listen to Mother Earth, here in the garden. Come quietly from time to time.

Through the quiet perhaps Mother Earth will speak of the tireless worms,

eaters of dirt and dying plants.

Worms—whose daily food weighs more than they do, and whose

bodies turn that food into rich soil to feed the growing garden.

Worms—who are like little plows, tunneling endlessly through the

earth to make room for air and water to feed the roots.

Worms—who work on through the winter, while most of us other gardeners rest.

Mother Earth loves these wet and crawling creatures, for whom we hold so

little affection. She reminds us that the worm is our brother.

Listen to Mother Earth, here in the garden.

Come quietly from time to time.

Come at sunrise when dewdrops greet the morning.

Come in sunshine, wind and rain.

Come to hear the crickets sing at dusk.

Come on a night lit up by the face of a full moon.

Come to the garden to honor the great and the small of life,

to love and be loved, to give and receive,

and always to grow and change.

Celebrating Life in the Garden

People throughout the ages and of many cultures have gathered in gardens to bless the seeds and the soil. In garden ceremonies people have called upon the gifts of the sun, rain, air, and earth, summoned the aid of divine beings, performed sacred dances, lifted up prayers in song, and celebrated great harvest festivals. The garden holds a compelling power over us, not only because it reminds us of our need for food to sustain our physical bodies, but also because it gives us dramatic evidence that in this life we are co-creators with unseen powers. In the garden, we begin to understand our deeper connections with the unseen, with the earth, and with one another.

The gardening celebrations which follow are meant to inspire your own creativity. When my spouse, Andrew, and I create celebrations for our family, we include appropriate songs, verses, or prayers, perhaps a folk tale or nature story, or a simple circle dance. With young children, it is helpful to keep verbal explanations brief. Simply guiding children through the celebration allows the experience to speak for itself.

Our Creative Kin: A Ground-Breaking Ceremony

After you have broken ground in the spring, gather to bless your garden. You may wish to celebrate what I call the "kindoms of creation" that together nurture the future harvest: the earth, the plants, the animals, and humanity. To celebrate the gifts of the earth, you might pass a bowl of rich soil, so each person can take a handful and spread it over the garden. To celebrate the gifts of the plants, you may have each person place some seedling markers into the garden plot, or do a bit of planting. To celebrate the animals, you could offer a box of earthworms to your garden. To celebrate human gifts you might pass a hoe or pitcher of water and allow each person to offer a symbolic gesture of tending to the garden's needs.

Sowing Our Visions: A Seed Blessing

Consider blessing your garden seeds before planting. Allow children to inspect the various types of seeds. Speak briefly of the wonder of these tiny seeds, which are planted into the soil and burst from their skins to sprout with new life. Speak of how these seeds are like the hopes we have for our lives—to learn to roller skate, make a new friend, or grow a healthy garden. Have each person plant some seeds to symbolize their vision for the future. Before each person waters their seeds, they can share their special hope. Consider writing these visions on the back of your garden markers.

The Gift of Garbage: Celebrating the Compost of Life

When you are experiencing a problem, use your compost pile as a positive symbol of change. Toss compost onto the pile (a bouquet of wilted flowers works well), and name your concerns about the trouble. Then speak briefly of the way the elements work together to change garbage into rich soil which helps the plants to grow. Affirm that troubles can also bring us unexpected gifts. Gather at the compost pile again in several weeks to consider what gifts have come out of your trouble. Perhaps someone has reached out to help you, or what seemed to be a problem was actually an opportunity to make a needed change. This ceremony is also useful in saying "good-bye" at such times as before a move, or after the death of a pet. Toss compost onto the pile and name the specific things that will be missed. Afterwards, turn the pile with a pitchfork or shovel and name your special memories, lessons, and gifts you have received from this place or pet. Allow everyone's thoughts and feelings to flow freely and honestly.

All Good Gifts: A Harvest Celebration

When you have gathered the last of your harvest (or perhaps the first fruits), consider celebrating an evening harvest ritual. Build a fire, tell stories, sing songs, dance together. Offer thanks to the earth, rain, air, and sun, as well as to the more invisible creative powers. Share memories of the changes and events experienced during the gardening season. Celebrate the harvest of your lives, as well as the harvest of the garden.

About the Author and Illustrator

Shea Darian grew up in Urbandale, Iowa. She received a B.A. in Speech Communications and Theater from Iowa State University, a Master of Divinity degree from Garrett-Evangelical Seminary, and trained in Waldorf school administration and community development at the Waldorf Institute of Sunbridge College. Shea is a writer, workshop leader, singer and songwriter. Her first book, *Seven Times the Sun: Guiding Your Child Through the Rhythms of the Day*, was published by LuraMedia in 1994. Shea lives in Brookfield, Wisconsin with her spouse, Andrew, and their daughters, Morgan and Willa.

Karlyn Holman's watercolors reflect a special exuberance for her native area of Lake Superior. Karlyn has an M.A. in art from the University of Wisconsin and has taught at the college level for twelve years. She is a full-time artist and owns Karlyn's Gallery. She teaches high-spirited watercolor workshops throughout the world. This is the third book that she has illustrated. Karlyn lives with her husband Gary in Washburn, Wisconsin.

Acknowledgments

I extend my heart-felt thanks to those who have helped to cultivate Grandpa's Garden: Lura Geiger, for the imaginative seed, Ana Cerro, for coaxing the story out of me, Maggie Jezreel, for her ideas and insights, Rebecca Danica, for the magic of her encouragement, Andrew, Morgan, and Willa Darian, who give me daily inspiration, my publisher, Bob Rinzler, for his expertise and his faith in this project, Glenn Hovemann, for his sensitive and insightful editing, Karlyn Holman, who has so lovingly brought these pages to life, and finally, my mother, Demetra Anne Woodyard, who has carried this story in her heart perhaps even longer than I. — *Shea Darian*

I would like to thank the following people who have made this illustrating adventure a reality: Brianna, my Mom and Keith Carlson for their joyful cooperation in being my models; Renee Holman for her constant encouragement and for finding Mr. Carlson and The Blue Vista Farm; Amy Kalmon for her help in photographing some of my reference materials; my many artist friends, especially Bonnie, Elisabeth, Jan, Mary, June, and Karen for sharing their references and their insightful comments; Shea Darian for her inspiring text and helpful suggestions regarding her visual conception for the book; Bob Rinzler for his faith in my abilities to illustrate the book; LeeAnn Brook for her creative talent in putting the book together. — *Karlyn Holman*